For Alice – JE

For Ioan – RH

MM

First published 2010 by Macmillan Children's Books
This edition published 2011 by Macmillan Children's Books
a division of Macmillan Publishers Limited
20 New Wharf Road, London N1 9RR
Basingstoke and Oxford
Associated companies throughout the world
www.panmacmillan.com

ISBN: 978-1-4472-0272-1

Text copyright © Jonathan Emmett 2010
Illustrations copyright © Rebecca Harry 2010
Moral rights asserted.
Find out more about Jonathan Emmett and Rebecca Harry's books at:
www.scribblestreet.co.uk
www.rebeccaharry.com

3 5 7 9 8 6 4

A CIP catalogue record for this book is available from the British Library.

Printed in China

Jonathan Emmett

Foxes in the Snow

Illustrated by Rebecca Harry

MACMILLAN CHILDREN'S BOOKS

In the middle of a forest, beneath the roots of an old oak tree, lived a family of foxes.

It was a cold winter's day, but Mother Fox was going out to look for food.

"Stay here in the den, where it's safe and snug," she told her two cubs.
And, with a flick of her tail, she was off into the forest.

Alfie and Bonnie snuggled down at the back
of the den. But Bonnie soon got bored.
"I'm going to look outside," she said.
"Remember what Mother told us," called Alfie.
"You mustn't leave the den."
"I'm just looking," said Bonnie.

Bonnie poked her nose outside and gasped
as something white and fluffy landed on it.

She tried to pick the fluffy
thing up, but it disappeared
as soon as she touched it.
"Alfie! Alfie! Come and
look!" she called.

The forest was filled with strange fluffy things.
They were falling through the air all around them.

"What are they?" asked Alfie.
"Whatever they are, I want one!" said Bonnie,
and they scrambled up and out of the den.

They forgot about staying safe and snug.
They forgot what Mother Fox had told them.

The two cubs jumped into the air,
trying to snap up the falling snowflakes.

"They melt in your mouth," said Alfie.

"They tickle your tongue," giggled Bonnie.

Through the trees they ran, laughing and
leaping through the whirling whiteness.

The snow was falling thick and fast now,
smothering the ground and covering the
branches, until the whole forest lay hidden
beneath a thick white blanket.

Suddenly Alfie stopped
and looked around him.
"Where are we?" he said.

They'd been having so much fun that they hadn't noticed where they were going. Now everywhere looked strange and unfamiliar. "I think we're lost," whimpered Bonnie.

Then Alfie had a brilliant idea!
"Look at our paw-prints," he said.
"We can follow them all
the way home!"

So back they went, noses to the ground,
tracing their tracks through the snow.

But it was getting late,
and the forest was getting darker . . .

and the paw-prints
grew fainter . . .

and fainter until . . .

. . . they disappeared completely.

"The snow must have filled them in," sniffed Bonnie.

Alfie and Bonnie huddled together.

The forest, which had felt so friendly, now felt cold and dangerous. And the two cubs wished that they had stayed safe and snug in their den, as Mother Fox had told them.

Crack!

Suddenly a twig snapped and the cubs caught a glimpse of something large running silently through the forest.

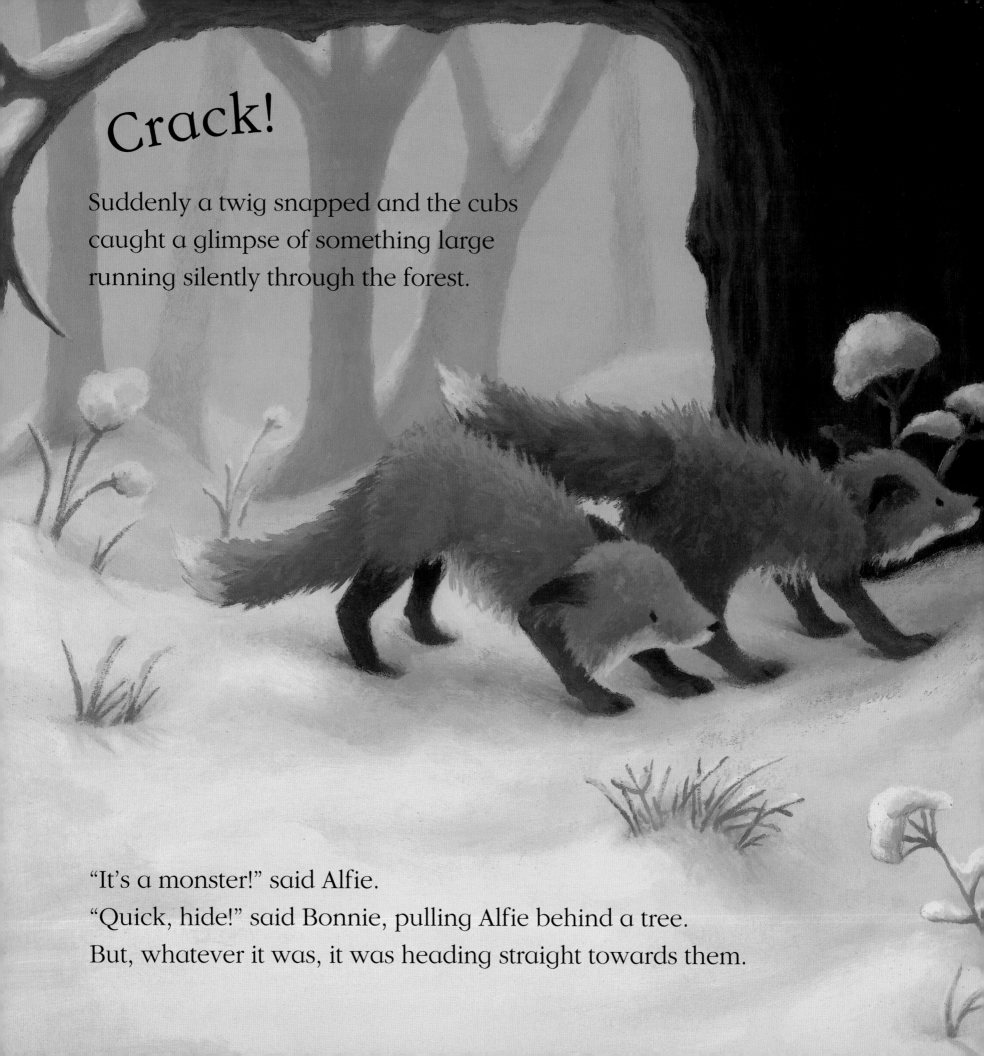

"It's a monster!" said Alfie.

"Quick, hide!" said Bonnie, pulling Alfie behind a tree.

But, whatever it was, it was heading straight towards them.

The two frightened cubs backed around the tree until . . .

Whoomph!

The snow gave way beneath them
and they tumbled down into a hole.
"Help!" cried Alfie. "What are we going to do?"
"I don't know," whimpered Bonnie.

Just then, a large shape appeared above them . . .

it was Mother Fox!

"Why do you look so scared?" she said.
"We didn't know it was you," gasped Alfie.
"How did you find us?" blurted Bonnie.
"Find you?" said Mother Fox. "But where
else would you be?"

Now everyone was puzzled, until
Alfie realised where they were.
"We're in the den!" he said.
"Of course!" said Mother Fox.
"Just as I left you."

It was a cold winter's evening, and Alfie and Bonnie were back in their den, beneath the roots of the old oak tree.

As the cubs finished their supper, Mother Fox told them
that they would have a big surprise in the morning.
"What sort of surprise?" asked Alfie.
"If I told you, it wouldn't be a surprise," said Mother Fox.

Alfie and Bonnie curled up sleepily together,
safe and snug, in the corner of the den.

"I think I know what sort of surprise it is," whispered Alfie.

"It's the sort that melts in your mouth."

"And tickles your tongue," giggled Bonnie.

"But I'm glad Mother Fox is coming too."